Francis Fontaine

The Exile: a Tale of St. Augustine

Francis Fontaine

The Exile: a Tale of St. Augustine

ISBN/EAN: 9783743340978

Manufactured in Europe, USA, Canada, Australia, Japa

Cover: Foto ©Andreas Hilbeck / pixelio.de

Manufactured and distributed by brebook publishing software
(www.brebook.com)

Francis Fontaine

The Exile: a Tale of St. Augustine

Dedication.

The signet of a woman's worth,
The truest test of gentle birth,
Is modesty :
The charm that links her to the sky,
The blossom that can never die !
Love forms the pure, sweet alchemy,
That leads the heart with sympathy
To perfect truth :
The Koh-i-noor, the brightest gem
In happy childhood's diadem.
My little child, may these traits bless
Thy innocence with joyousness
And gentleness :
For modesty, and love, and truth,
Alike in childhood, age or youth
Make happiness.

INTRODUCTION.

The history of Florida, the most ancient of the American colonies, is replete with romance, and, among all the legends connected therewith, none equals in thrilling interest the subject of this poem.

The early settlement of St. Augustine, the oldest town in the United States, forms the basis of this story, which essays to delineate one of the most horrible massacres in the annals of history.

The spirit which animated the French Catholics to murder their compatriots of the Huguenot faith, on St. Bartholomew's eve, inspired the Spaniards, under the Adelantado Menendez, to commit a like atrocity at Fort Caroline, near St. Augustine, Florida.

Historical accuracy is not claimed for the poem ; but, that the reader may understand the narrative, I have translated a part of the " mémoire " of Francisco Lopez de Mendoza, chaplain of the Spanish expedition under Menendez : and also alluded to a similar narration by one of the survivors of the Huguenot colony.

MEMOIRE.

"De l'heureux résultat et du bon voyage que Dieu, notre Seigneur, a bien voulu accorder à la flotte qui partit de la ville de Cadiz pour se rendre à la côte et dans la province de la Floride, et dont était général l'illustre Seigneur Pedro Menendez de Aviles, commandeur de l'ordre de Saint Jacques. Cette flotte partit de la baie de Cadiz le jeudi matin 28 du mois de juin 1565 ; elle arriva sur les côtes des provinces de la Floride le 28 août de la même année."

PAR FRANCISCO LOPEZ DE MENDOZA,
Chapelain de l'expédition.

"Your Excellency will remember that when I was in Spain I went to see the General at the port Saint Marie, and that he showed me a letter from Monseigneur the King Don Philip, signed by his hand, in which His Majesty stated, that on the 20th of May, the same year, seven French ships, bearing seven hundred men and two hundred women, had sailed for Florida." (Then follows a description of the armament of the Spanish fleet, and the instructions given to the Adelantado Pedro Menendez to proceed to Florida and claim the country for the King of Spain. *Translator.*)

"On the eighth of the month, the day of the nativity of Our Lady, the General landed with many banners displayed, to the sound of trumpets and of other instruments of war, and amid salvos of artillery. I took a cross and went before them chanting *Te Deum Laudamus.* The General marched straight to the cross, followed by all those who accompanied him : they knelt and kissed the cross. A great many Indians witnessed the ceremonies and imitated all that they saw done. The same day the General took possession of the country in the name of His Majesty. All the Captains swore allegiance to him as their General, and as Adelantado of the country.

* * * * * * * *

"We are in this fort to the number of six hundred combatants.

* * * * * * * *

" To-day, as I finished the mass of Our Lady, the Admiral was informed that a Frenchman had been captured. He told us that our enemies had embarked more than two hundred men on four vessels to go in search of our fleet ; God our Father sent suddenly so great a tempest that these men must have been destroyed, for since their departure have occurred the worst tempests I ever saw.

" The following Monday we saw a man approach who cried out loudly : ' Victory ! Victory ! the French fort is in our hands !' I have already stated that the enterprise which we have undertaken is for the glory of Jesus Christ and of His Holy Mother. The Holy Spirit has enlightened the reason of our chief, in order that all may be turned to our profit and that we might gain so great a victory. The enemy did not perceive them until they were attacked, most of them being in bed ; many arose in their night-clothes and begged for quarter. Notwithstanding this, one hundred and forty-two were killed ; the rest escaped. In an hour's time the fort was in our possession.

" A few days after this, some Indians came to our fort and informed us, by signs, that a French vessel had been wrecked on Anastasia Island. The General, with the Admiral and many followers repaired to the coast and, taking with him a Frenchman who had accompanied us from Spain, he called to them to come over. A French gentlemen who was a serjeant, brought their reply to the summons to surrender—for they had raised a flag as a signal of war— he said that they would surrender on condition that their lives might be spared. The General demanded an unconditional surrender. Seeing that no other resource remained to them, in a short time they all surrendered themselves to his discretion. Seeing that they were Lutherans, his Excellency condemned them all to death ; but, as I was a priest and felt a sympathy for them, I begged him to grant me a favor : that of sparing those who would embrace our holy faith. He granted me this favor ; I succeeded in thus saving ten or twelve ; all the rest were executed because they were Lutherans and enemies of our holy Catholic faith. All this took place on the day of Saint Michael, September 22, 1565. There were one hundred and eleven Lutherans executed, without counting fourteen or fifteen prisoners."

I, Francisco Lopez de Mendoza Grajales, Chaplain of his Excellency, certify that the foregoing is true.

FRANCISCO LOPEZ DE MENDOZA GRAJALES.

A Huguenot survivor of the attack on Fort Caroline has described that human butchery as, "a massacre of men, women and little infants, so horrible that one can imagine nothing more barbarous and cruel."

He also states, in his *mémoire*, that the number of the French in the Fort, including the women and children, was two hundred and forty souls; the rest having embarked on the vessels sent in search of the Spanish fleet, which vessels were wrecked in the storm. Of the two hundred and forty persons in the Fort, one hundred and eleven were slain, according to the statement of the Catholic Mendoza. The Fort was attacked while the Huguenots were asleep. It is upon this massacre that this poem is founded.   F. F.

THE EXILE.

A TALE OF SAINT AUGUSTINE.

DRAMATIS PERSONÆ.

RENÉ DE LAUDONNIÈRE, { *Commandant at Fort Caroline, and Commander of the Huguenots.*

JEAN RIBAULT, . . . *Captain of the French Fleet.*

LÉONORE DE COLIGNY, { *Daughter of Admiral Coligny, and affianced to Count Ribault.*

NICOLAS DE CHALLEUX, . *Chaplain of the Huguenots.*

DUC DE ROHAN,
DOMINIQUE DE GOURGUES, } *Huguenot Captains.*

Soldiers, Sailors and Colonists.

PEDRO MENENDEZ DE AVILES, *Adelantado for the King of Spain, and Commander of the Spaniards.*

MOSCOSO, ... *Lieutenant to the Adelantado.*

MENDOZA, ... *Chaplain to the Catholics.*

FATHER CORPA, . . . *A Faithful Catholic Missionary.*

Spanish Soldiers, Sailors and Colonists.

COACOOCHEE, . . *Chief of the Seminole Indians.*

THRONATISKA, . *An Indian Maiden affianced to Coacoochee.*

Indians, Men and Women.

"STAND ·Fetlock!" he said, and his horse which
    had reared
When the galloping sound of a fleet courser neared
The smiling *bosquet*, now but pricks forth its ears
As the challenging neigh of a rival it hears.
She did not know him, only saw him as he sat
Like a seeming centaur; but he lifted his hat
As she passed fleetly by near the edge of the wood
Where his steed champed its bit as it loyally stood.
"—Stand Fetlock!" then he smiled as he witnessed
    the sight,
For her horse and its burden seemed as one in the
    flight.

The soft air was balmy, and the sky was serene
As a lake as she rode 'neath the far-reaching green
Of the Bois de Boulogne with her father, that day,
In the free *nonchalance* of a child when at play.
With laughter, that rippled like a stream on the
    sand
In musical cadence, and a wave of the hand,
She galloped forth fleetly 'neath the summer-green
    trees

Up the wide avenue, while the frolicsome breeze
Played havoc with tresses that floated away
Like the floss of the silk on a mid-summer day.

"—She is the fairest and loveliest maid of the
North," Said the young Cavalier when the maiden
    rode forth ;
So winsome, so naïve, that he looked with delight
As the fair equestrienne, like a star in its flight
'Cross the blue vault of heaven, sped on—and away—
And Fetlock, impatient, replied with a neigh.

More than one, yes full many, sought to aid her to
    keep
The horse in the course but, repelled by the sweep
Of the fair maiden's hand, admiring, withdrew
As she passed like a meteor on—on in their view.
More than all, he admired, when with magical
    grace—
While the soft hue of health suffused her bright face
And her tresses floated back, by the wind uncon-
    fined,—
He saw her, all fearlessly, draw the quick rein
And return with the speed of the tempest again.

Her father enjoyed it : for he knew that his child,

Reared most of her life in the bold rugged wild
Of her own Moncontour, was as safe in that seat
As you maidens from Paris who have sought this
    retreat
For a day in the country: who think that they here
See its splendor and beauties, and breathe the pure
    air
Of the God-given country; but devices of art
Near a great crowded city cannot pleasures impart,
Such as Nature doth give in the land o'er the sea:
The home of the homeless and the pride of the free!

Lakes there vie with the ocean, and snow-peaks in
    the skies
There charm the bold eagle, which right royally flies
On the wings of the wind till 'tis lost to the eyes;
Then it lights, like the chamois, on the high alpen-
    height
Where dry snow whirls like dust; and it screams
    with delight
As the storm rages 'neath him; while the bright
    heavens seem
The mystical opening of an angelic dream.
Thus it seemed to Coligny, who offered his hand
To the gallant young Count, whom he had seen lead
    a band
In the cavalry charge, when the arquebuse rattle

And the hot cannonade of the fiercely fought battle
Had littered the field with the wounded and dead
Whence all save Coligny and his squadron had fled.
Now their meeting, though sudden, was cordial and
    brief   ·
When the young Count de Ribault saluted his chief.

But the maiden had neared them with slow-pranc-
    ing steed
Which, with nostrils expanded, had slackened its
    speed.
" —My daughter—Count Ribault." She blushed, as
    the name
Of the gallant young captain so well-known to fame
Was pronounced by her father, and bowed in re-
    sponse ;
Thus they met, thus parted, with a bow and a glance.

*   *   *   *   *   *   *   *

" —She's as fair as the flowers that bloom in her hair,
Unadorned save by these —yes exquisitely fair ! "
Thus he spake as he saw her at the Elysée ball,
For she danced with the grace of a swan on a lake
And her smile was as pure as the falling snow-flake,

When she moved like a queen in the slow minuet.
While he twirled in his hand a sweet mignonette.

.

But a swarthy face frowned, when De Guise saw the
    sight
Of the lovers, who danced in the palace that night—
And 'twas plain they were lovers, despite the dis-
    guise
Of a formal acquaintance, for Count Ribault's eye,
As the needle follows magnet, her figure descries
Wherever it is seen ; while Léonore's face
Acknowledged with blushes this homage to grace—

The two rival suitors were acquainted, but when
They met on this evening they met as do men
Who know not each other, and, with proud haughty
    air,
Count Ribault returned the Duke's insolent stare.
Yet 'twas a thorn to his love, and a spur to his
    pride
When he saw the proud De Guise at Léonore's side ;
And the thorn rankled deep, as the Count thought
    of all
The sneering allusions of the Duke at the ball.

Days, weeks, and months passed, when Count Ri-
    bault one day,

As the shadows of twilight enveloped with gray
The great gilded city, ere the lamp-lights were lit,
Told her father he had loved her since first he had
     met
The Lady Léonore in the Bois de Boulogne,
And no one heard Count Ribault save Coligny
     alone.

"—My child's happiness is more than all else to me
And I know that her heart has been given to thee.
But, Count Ribault, I fear that an hour may bring
An end to this truce and sound the tocsin again,
I trust not the promise of a treacherous king.
Should it happen—and should this city be the scene
Where the old and the helpless are ruthlessly slain ;
Should our people then rise to revenge them again,
Unfurl once again that flag which they've borne
In the days when the Huguenots learned how to
     mourn
All armed for the fray : 'tis my wish—nay command,
That Léonore shall go to that far sunny land
Where such crimes are unknown, and the fierce iron
     hand
Of Civil War cannot come ; to that land, where the
     sun
Lends its most genial rays to the soft Southern air,
And freights the cool breezes deliciously there ;

Where it dimples the waves of the clearest of
    streams—
The matchless Welaka.* Promise this, and her hand
Shall go with her heart to that sweet Southern land."

Thus 'twas settled—yet not settled—

Like a rosy-fingered bride come the first tints of
    dawn
Enwreathing with orange the clouds, while the fawn
Shakes the dew from its flanks, and the wild flowers
    feast,
And the birds carol forth their hymns to the East.

Afar o'er the hills sounds the loud-ringing horn
Of the hunter who rides in the crisp early morn.
Flee Reynard ! though weary, continue thy flight,
For Aurora is belting the world with its light ;
And the moon slowly sinks down the vale of the
    night ;
      For the great sun advances
      From the realm of the night,
      With its dazzling light-lances,
      With its sharp spears of light

---

* Indian name of the St. John's river.

Over the sky, over the earth, and the sea:
Flee away to thy covert—away—flee away !

As the stars of the night faded one after one
From the crimsoning skies till the last star was gone,
So the timid little hares fled fast from the morn,
But Reynard stood listening the notes of the horn.

While the harebells and daisies were crushed 'neath
   the feet
Of the horses and hounds as they coursed to "the
   meet "
Till their dew-cups ran o'er, yet Reynard stood still
Like a sentinel watching from the brow of the hill.
On the air of the morn sounds again the loud horn
And the eager fox-hounds fill the air with their
   sounds;
Now Reynard is gone—like the wind he has flown !
While the loud yelping pack follows close on his
   track,
So fleetly, so hotly, that he dares not look back !
Through the field and the forest, speeding fleetly
   alone,
Crossing fences with briars and brambles overgrown,
Swimming streams and crossing gullies, poor Rey-
   nard at last,

With his tongue hanging out and his sides panting
    fast,
Turns back on his course, and with footsteps as
    fleet
As the wide prairie wind, enters quick his retreat.

See the gay cavalcade! there, all flushed with de-
    light,
Rides the fair Léonore keeping Reynard in sight,
While her escort, with a brief "*au revoir!*" makes
    detour
Around the deep forest which skirts Moncontour.

With the pride of an heiress on her own native heath
Léonore rides alone in the green forest wild
Where the high clambering vines festoon and en-
    wreath
The tall forest trees—where she played when a
    child.
Léonore rides alone; for each path's as well known
To the fearless young maiden, as if 'twas her own.
Unharmed by the woodman, the fox and the deer
Roam their own native wilds in security here,
Save when the fair mistress is *en-route* for the chase,
When the horn of the hunter awakens the place
Where Reynard reclines, till its echoes awake
The wild solitude of fen, thicket, and brake.

From a copse in the wood, where wild squirrels ran
    free
Without fear and unthreatened, up and down a
    great tree,
While the fair maiden smiled, mounted troopers
    rushed forth
Seized her horse by the rein and turned its head to
    the North.
In a moment 'twas done! one scream and no more,
For swiftly and silently they bore Léonore
A captive away! while sounds of the chase
Grew dimmer and dimmer as they quickened their
    pace.

  * * * * * *

Moncontour is grief-stricken : fast assemble a host
To hear the sad tidings.   Its heiress is lost !
And the Lord of the castle, Coligny, is slain !
And his tenants seem eager to don armor again.
Dark grow the swarthy brows, closer clench yeo-
    man hands
Of the men here assembled at Count Ribault's com-
    mands ;
One word from thee Ribault will, like match to the
    pine,
Enflame all these souls with a vengeance like thine!

Not a moment was lost! up the hills, down the vale,
Despite the fierce rumblings that portend a gale,
On, onward they go! still pursuing the trail
Till the smoke from the village, now far in their
    rear,
Tells the young chieftain's band that the foemen
    are there!
Now the swarthy cheeks blanched, for yon lurid,
    red fire,
Which flames from their homes, sees their children
    expire!
Then a combat ensues; though they fight long and
    well
They fight against fate, and they see the black
    plume
Of their gallant young chieftain fall!—As he fell,
It seemed like the knell of the Huguenot's doom
And they yielded at last as the tree to the blast.

Moncontour is *en deuil*. Moncontour, Moncontour!
Take down thy proud banner, and hang crape at
    thy door;
For thy halls are as silent as the grave of thy Lord;
Let the harp of Æolus now alone touch the chord!

Thy yeomen, where are they? Moncontour, Mon-
    contour!

Nought remains of their dwellings but the charred
    ashen floor,
And the smoke which ascends from yon cot to high
    heaven
Shows how thy poor tenants from their homes have
    been driven.

Thy chieftains have fallen 'neath the false-hearted
    blow
Of a wily and craven and treacherous foe;
But again thy bold banner floats proudly and free
On the mast of a vessel sailing outward to sea.
And a maiden is led by the captain away
From the deck to the bridge. The old captain is
    gray,
But his weather-tanned face shows that Laudonnière
Is a stout-hearted friend and a stranger to fear.
The bravest are the gentlest, and the weak and for-
    lorn
To the strongest and truest instinctively turn
In the hour of trial—when a look from the eye
And a clasp of the hand speak the heart's sympa-
    thy.
Thus his look, thus his clasp, as he led her that day
And pointed to the shores fast fading away.

"Look! look Léonore! see those hills on the
    shore—

See, between them, yon castle—'tis thy own Mon-
    contour!
The turrets, like grim sentinels, are watching the
    flight
Of the vessel which takes thee, an exile, from sight.
Bear up bravely, my child! thou wilt yet again be
Yon castle's proud mistress, though we cross now
    the sea ;
There thy ancestral flag shall float proudly and free,
And thy tenantry again shout welcome to thee."

Then he ceased, and she looked, while her lovely
    cheeks blanched
And her eyes filled with tears, and her hands were
    close-clenched ;
Yet she said not a word, but the gaze of her eyes
Lingered longingly there till the shores seemed the
    skies.
But the changing-hued waters tossed upward white
    spray
While the Huguenot vessel ploughed onward its
    way.
Now the shore-lines are gone: white, blue, or deep
    green
The waves of the ocean are the only things seen
Save the gulls, and the hues of the horizon sky,
As the fair hills of Normandy fade from the eye.

That very day the Spanish fleet
Cast anchor near Saint Augustine;
And standards sway, while music sweet
From gay-decked vessels charm the scene.
And lances, halberds and breast-plates gleam
Athwart a ship which rides the stream
As lightly as a swan would swim.
Then deftly sailors plume its wings,
And then a standard upward flings
Its bunting to the breeze.

Aurora's soft prismatic tints
Had traced the skies where nature prints
The fleecy forms which drift away
Like phantom ships on azure sea;
And now the sun-light, glancing, gave
To whitened beach and shining wave
Resplendent hues. With martial mien
A moving host adds to the scene,
Proud banners bear, and arms of war,
And now upon this foreign shore
They plant the holy cross.

And naked natives, in bark canoe
Rowed in and out while white curlew
And long-billed crane, and wild-duck fly
With wonderment from marsh to marsh;

And parrots speak, with accents harsh,
And Indians view with curious stare
These horses, arms, and men.

Now closer grouped the natives round
The point which severs sea and river,
When lo! the shifting dazzling quiver
Of sun-light on the flashing swords
Of men who crowd yon vessel's boards
Is seen.   Gleam helmets rich and rare
And sun-bright shields, which those who dare
The mightiest feats of valor, wear.

These simple natives then were free—
Sole owners of this land and sea,
Save the old town of Augustine
Which claimed allegiance to Spain—
Nor feared they aught from these strange men
Who marched with flaunting banners then;
But Indians grasped the Spanish hand
As fast as Spaniards reached the land,
For they were friendly; yes as kind
And unsuspecting as you'll find
In any race beneath the sun,
Ere white men, for ambitious goal—
The lust of power—had begun
A crusade 'gainst the Seminole!

As Spaniards glanced from clear blue skies
To tropic scenes which charmed their eyes—
To where the graceful tall bananas
Slow-waved their great wide leaves, like banners;
To where the bushy youpon grew,
And cluster-berries of shining hue,
While sweet perfumes from crab-wood trees
Freighted each passing scented breeze;
From Indian brave with wampum belt,
To Indian maid with deerskin kilt
That showed beneath, the rounded limb,
Above, the arm, as round and trim,
And bronze bosom plump, full, and fair—
A wild huzza loud rent the air.

The foliage seemed a sea of green
And ev'ry tree a separate scene;
The woods as tinted o'er with gold
When sun-light pierced the thicket fold.
They saw a glimpse of silver thread,
As streamlet gushed from fountain head;
And lovely birds of plumage gay
Flitted and sang the live-long day;
But now they ceased their morning lay
And fluttered to the copse-wood green,
Or winged their way far from the scene.
Even that bird of wondrous hue,

Whose tiny form so rapid flew
From flower to flower—as gay
As any sun-beam of the day—
Affrighted by the *vivas* loud,
Now swiftly flew into the wood.

Helvetia boasts its lofty heights
All clad in Alpine robe of snow;
Fair Florida the balmy nights
When stars gleam in the depths below
The mirrored surface of a Spring,
Where mighty ships can anchors swing
And freely turn, although a fleet
Another squadron there might meet.

—" Arcadian dream, nor painter's brush
Has ere depicted sylvan hush
More sweetly wild than is this scene
In far-off Florida, I ween!"
Thus thought the maiden, who looked into
The clear blue depths—so deep and clear
That many fathoms seemed anear,
Where swimming fish like silver gleam—
Now here, now there along the stream.

There, many a silver streamlet wakes
Winding its way to the chain of lakes

That forms the famed Welaka, and there
Sing birds, of plumage gay and rare;
While wild-wood sweets perfume the air.
And there, tradition waves its wand
As if this were enchanted land—
So many and so wild the tales
With which it treats these sylvan vales.

The exiles wonder when they see
Engraved on rock or carved on tree
The emblems of idolatry:
Idols, that bear on face and breast
Good evidence that 'twas the East—
Not North or South—that to the West
Gave birth to preëxistent creeds
On which the mind untutored feeds—
They do not kneel, nor do they pray
To God or man, but earnestly
Clasp hands up to yon glowing sun
When first its lances crest the sea,
And then again when it goes down
And slowly, grandly pales away.

The exiles see the Phallic symbol—
A stag upon a branchless tree—
Rude carved, 'tis true, but plain to see—
Which proved that on this rounded cone

Peru's old heliolatry
Had 'stablished worship of the Sun.
Concentric paths led round and up
Until it reached the utmost top,
Where savages were wont to make
Their offerings of human blood—
As sacrifice to heathen god.

There stood alone upon the shore
The exile maiden—and Lénore
Seemed fearless as an Indian maid;
For there the savage hand was stayed
Because this ancient Phallic mound
Was deemed by them as holy ground.
The trees soft zephyrs gently stir,
And now she hears the rapid whir
Of partridge as it flies past her
From shore to shore and out of sight,
Then cries to her "Good night!" "good night!"

Its cry was answered by a dove
Whose cooing accents spake of love,
And bore her thoughts to France again,
—"Is Ribault captive, or is he slain?"
She thought of him, whose fearless eye
Was pregnant with true chivalry;
For truth had signet-stamped with grace

On brow, and eyes, and gailant face
Its seal of noble, knightly mien—
His stalwart form showed manliness,
His smile showed valor, gentleness,
And none but bravest knights could share
The plume which he was wont to wear
When he appeared in knightly list
Where only valor's sons contest.
His guerdon was her love: his prize
The smile that blessed his longing eyes:
His creed was chivalry's behest:
To help the weak; with arms resist
The tyrant Might; by force remove
Oppressive wrong; and kneel to love.

He had not sought by courtier's art
To win this lovely maiden's heart,
But in the lists no braver knight
More gallantly struck down his foe,
Nor parried with a stronger might
Some skilful knight's titanic blow.
But 'twas not this, nor courtier's art,
But manliness which won her heart,
And where was he? Alas! the past
Was filled with joys that could not last.

Not now did servants, with watchful eye
To do her bidding linger nigh;
Nor were proud courtiers bending near
" My Lady's" least accents to hear;
Nor could she see the mullioned windows,
The castle's turrets, or gray old walls
Where ivy vines and roses clamber;
Nor walk her own ancestral halls—
In dreams alone she, smiling, wanders
Back to those days of joy and ease—
In dreams alone sees scenes like these.

She saw cloud-castles in the skies
And mountain-peaks, so snowy white
It seemed profane for amber dies,
To put those fleecy clouds to flight;
She saw these snowy shapes roll on
Like fairy forms, far down beneath
The lake-like surface, where the sun
Burnished the rippling waves, until
'Twas hidden by yon tree-clad hill.

She turned her head and, lo! a bear
Nosed close the ground and hovered near,
While near yon thicket, too, a deer
With branching antlers did appear:
She trembled then—as doth the hare,

In covert crouching low with fear,
While hunter's hound and hunter's face
Peer all around and near the place—
Then saw it rise and sudden wing
A feathered arrow 'cross the spring!
What seemed a bear, what seemed a deer
Were savage Indians lurking there!
But, soon as ribbon white was seen,
The Indians vanished in the green;
Nor twang of bow, nor rifle shot
Was ever meant for Huguenot.

Not conquest brought the exiles there,
Nor did they come as foes, but share,
With those who owned the continent,
Their little all, and rest content.
But Catholics did gloat upon
This fairy land, where tropic sun
Hath made a banquet free to all,
Resolved to make all others fall.
The Spaniards made these Indians foes,
For Indians knelt 'neath Spanish blows
Of lash or sword, or fell when fire
From arquebuse bade slaves 'expire!

The birds that now so blithesomely
Twittered and sing from tree to tree,

Bring back her thoughts to him again.
Whose life had been like summer day,
Until war's rude alarums bade
The kindly youth to draw his blade,
And lead his squadron to the fray
With waving sword, and ringing cheer
That all his troopers loved to hear.

The stars were witness when one night
His raven hair with golden met;
And sun-bronzed face of ruddy hue
Met lily cheeks: and eyes of blue
Looked up to his which looked again.
—" Is he a captive, or is he slain ? "
The twigs were bent, an Indian maid,
Like elfin fay at edge of wood,
Approached her from the woodland glade.
The nut-brown maid now silent stood,
Plump as a partridge, and as shy
And brown as the thrush which flitted by—
The daisy bowed, then raised its head
Unharmed by this brown maiden's tread ;
And bowed, unhurt, the violet
When these two girls in silence met.

At last she said to Léonore,
In Indian tongue—and then by signs—

Pointing the while to boat and oar :
" I've come from where the white beach sands
Receive and clasp the ocean's hands ;
Like autumn leaves thy friends will fall
An they heed not the Brown Thrush's call.
Like winter's gale the foemen come,
To spoil the White Magnolia's bloom,
If I can not excite her fears ;
The forest is alive with spears
That rise and sway like marsh-arrows,
And the river bristles with canoes ;
The Spaniards come ! As are the leaves
Or countless stars, so are their braves,
Who come with swords and arquebuse
And cannon, and with subtle ruse
Meant only to deceive—As slaves
The Spaniards treat our free-born braves !
Like sands in numbers are their men,
Who treat as carrion the slain !
I've come to warn—my task is done,
For ere to-morrow's rising sun
Shall spear the clouds with slanting rays,
The White Magnolia's blooming days
Will end forever more."

    But Léonore,
Who could not understand the maid,
With kindly smile then shook her head.
Again she spoke—made signs again—

Then, seeing that all words were vain
She sorrowfully turned away,
Drew up her boat, then seized the oar
And, stepping in, pushed off from shore.
Then rowed to where stood Léonore
And begged her to escape once more,
But all in vain : with saddened face,
The Indian maid rowed from the place.

She watched her form bend to the oar
Till dimpled knee was seen no more;
The vision passed almost as soon
As passing cloud unveils the moon ;
As flashing oar went from her sight
The evening sun in Western sky
Slow-reddened till a crimson dye
O'erspread the heavens with paling light.
The willows stooped to kiss the stream
Which rippled 'neath the sun-set gleam,
As Thronatiska passed from view ;
And twilight darkened now the hue
Of earth and sky, ere Léonore
Had left the placid lake-like shore.

The distant " tattoo" sounds to rest
And ev'ry bird hath sought its nest
Save black-winged bat, which here and there

Sweeps down or circles in the air.
Deep darkness veils the earth and sky :
The pine trees bow, while night-winds sigh,
And needles from their summits tall
Sway gracefully, then, noiseless, fall.

Yon ship, which proudly walks the sea
With canvass spread, while jauntily
A pennon floats from tallest mast
And hundreds view, from yonder shore,
Their comrades nearing home at last,
Spreads sails until there are no more :
It seems indeed a jubilee !
For canvass breasts the bracing breeze
With seeming pride, as if the seas
Were subject to the vessel's sway,
Not vessel subject to the seas.
One mother there seems tearful-sad,
While all the rest seem joyous-glad,
They mind her not, but careless seem :
Last night *she* dreamed a fearful dream.

The gale ! the gale ! the vessel creaks,
While billows roar 'mid wildest shrieks,
And England's cliffs shuts out the scene.
An hour ago the sun was bright
And hundreds gaily viewed the scene

As vessel spread, like bird, its wings,
And friends on shore cried welcomings.
Again the sea lashes sides and ends,
Leaps over gunwales, then descends
With savage roar : the ship careens
Amid the most heartrending scenes !

It fights the sea like thing of life
Battling against unequal strife ;
With sails all set it breaks, and then
Goes down with all its stores and men !
Like a culprit the tide has fled,
The ocean yields us back our dead
And launches them upon the sands :
Yon upturned face, close clenched hands,
And stiffened form, show sadly where
That mother's son lies lifeless there !
Like ghastly phantom on her brain
A dream last night portrayed this scene.

To dream—what is it then to dream ?
To live our happy youth again,
Or view the heart's acutest pain ?
To foretell, with prophetic ken
The future of our fellow-men ?
To read, like twinkling of a star,
The future in a dream ?   To mar

Or make one's happiness, the theme
Of sleeping thoughts in wakeful dream?

A dream, what is a dream?   A horoscope
Like birth of grief or death of hope?
A photograph of life—a mirror
Making to-day seem as to-morrow?
A tale of bliss—a scene of horror
Foretelling what is past?   Is this
A dream in its analysis?

    *   *   *   *   *   *

The goddess, Sleep, smiled gently o'er
The dreaming thoughts of Léonore.

HER DREAM.

Sweet is the perfume of the meadows—
The aroma of the new-mown hay;
For the harvesters raked the green clover
And turned it in the sun-shine to-day,
It sweetens the breezes of evening
As they come from the meadows to me,
And I hear, in the distance, the lowing
Of cattle as they scent the sweet hay.

For brown-tipped and sweet was the clover
When the harvesters cut it to-day,
And they turned it all over and over
Then piled it in hay-cocks away;
They piled it for fear that the shadows
Or the night-dew might dampen the hay,
And freight me its sweets from the meadow,
With the fragrance half wasted away.

Above me are swaying the blossoms
That now sweeten the summer-clad tree,

And I list to the lowing of cattle
That belong to my love and to me.
Sweet roses of Summer are blooming
While sun-set makes russet the hills,
And I hear from the village the chiming
Of the musical Normandy bells.

But sweeter than roses of summer
Or the song of the harvesters free ;
And sweeter than is the aroma
From the sweet-scented newly-mown hay,
Or the vines that embrace the old castle,
Or the deep silver lake that I see ;
And sweeter than lowing of cattle,
Is the voice of my lover to me.

Last eve as I walked in the gloaming
Near the beautiful clear silver spring,
Which placidly sleeps near the castle,
To the haunts where the mocking-birds sing,
I heard the dear voice of my lover
Coming out from the garden to me,
For the great banquet hall was fast filling
While I stood 'neath the blossoming tree.

" Léonore ! Léonore ! my darling,
The guests now await us in the hall,

In the hall where dark figures in armor
Guard ancestral portraits on the wall :
The guests all arrayed for the banquet,
Are patiently waiting my bride."
Then I saw him—my husband—my lover—
Gazing on me with fondness and pride.

But lo! the dream was snapped in twain,
The dreamer heard now shrieks of pain,
And arquebuse and fatal stroke
Of sword, and battle-axe awoke
The hapless Léonore.　　As form
The massing cloud-clans for the storm,
To march in columns o'er the plain
And sweep the earth with hail and rain—
As doth the cyclone's tempest wrath
Mow down the forest in its path
And leaves not a shrub—so the foe
With ruthless hands, sows seeds of woe
Where all was peace before.

Alas! ere startled men can rise
And seize their arms, they hear the cries
Of Spanish foes without the walls :
And soon the arquebuse's rattle,
As foemen charge, proclaims a battle ;

And soon the dreadful scene appals!
For children vainly seek to flee,
And maidens sink beneath the knee
Of ruffians, who scorn the prayer
Of those who kneel in vain despair;
One fatal stroke and maiden dies,
While mother, clasping infant, flies!

But hark! there sounds a bugle blast
That stops the fugitives at last;
There waves above a chieftain's head
A tall black plume, and near, the dead
Around his feet show that the might
Of this old gray-haired, dauntless knight
Hath made these doughty Spaniards know
His stalwart strength and giant blow.
Nor weight of axe, nor leaden hail
Could pierce, it seemed, his coat of mail;
'Twas made of finest chains; nor steel
Nor arquebuse, nor gleaming spear
Could make this valiant chieftain kneel,
Nor halbard harm Laudonnière.

" Shame on ye men! why do ye fly?
Strike for your lives, like brave men die!
Coligny! to the rescue!"
As eagle sweeps from aerie high

With maddened clutch upon its prey;
As panther leaps from limb of tree
Forewarning with its human cry:
So rushed the Huguenots that day,
As tigers spring, as lions slay!

And by that slogan hundreds formed
And forced back those who vainly stormed,
Till, foremost in the fierce contest,
Was seen the lofty waving crest
Of Menendez. Two bright swords flashed
As leaders met and steel blades clashed.

A whoop! a whirl of sabres there
As charging squadrons shake the air!
DeRohan's column thundered on
And forced them back, until but one
Was left to face Laudonnière.
And yet Menendez showed no fear:
Success with him meant honor, life;
Defeat to him meant death in strife:
And never yet did two men fight
With stronger nerves, or braver might.

Each gave—returned the Titan blow,
Each found his foe a worthy foe,
And parried with such knightly skill

That flames seemed glancing from the steel.
Now each advances, then retires
Resolved to fight till one expires:
Now one has made a mighty thrust,
And one lies prostrate in the dust !

The combat ceased : and Laudonnière
Leaned on his sword, as if to rest,
For faintly cheering caught his ear
As Spaniards flee.   A deep red trace
Across that bold gray-bearded face
Had left its seal—an honored scar—
The record of most valiant war !
Which showed that death had barely spared
The life which he so bravely dared.

He raised his visor then, to breathe
The fresh crisp air,—placed sword in sheathe,
Then wound a long, shrill bugle blast
And mounted horse to leave at last—
But lingered :—afar he heard the sound
Of pursuers and of pursued ;
Anear, and scattered o'er the ground,
The dead and dying close he viewed :
This form the mangled corse of one
Whose battle deeds alas ! are done ;
And that a mother clasping fast
An infant to her frozen breast !

—" Fold little hands! close little eyes in sleep,
Death's angel calls—none need for thee to weep!"
Thus spake Laudonnière, and then
He saw upturned a gentle face
Which senseless lay without a trace
Of life; and then he knelt before
The senseless form of Léonore.

—" So fair, so young, so beautiful!
Art thou, too, slain, my child, my all!
Slain by a dastard! cruel foe
Who shamed his kind by this fell blow!
Ah! woe is me! alas!
That I should see the bleeding tress;
This senseless form, whose lovely grace
Even in death is beautiful!
That I should see this pallid face
And learn, too late, that thou wert all,
Aye! *all* indeed, that gave to life
Its charm—and yet, as Ribault's wife
Thou woulds't be lost to me. Sweet eyes!
Unclose thy gentle lids and see
How thou art all in all to me!"
He held her in his arms; caressed
Her gently, and as gently kissed
The pallid lips;—once, twice, *again*—
He strained her to his breast.

He bowed his head upon her head
And groaned, though foes attack the glade
Where Huguenots await their chief
Who thinks no more of them ; who hears
But listens not ; nor heeds the fears
Which erst oppressed him most, that they
Would fail to hold their own that day.

As climbs the vine around the tree,
With gentle clasp, and tenderly,
So had this maiden claimed a part,
Then all, of the old chieftain's heart.
She knew it not ; she little dreamed
That he was not that which he seemed :
That which he vowed he longed to be
The day when, pointing from the sea
To France, he said : " Thy father's friend
My child, until thy life shall end
Shall henceforth be thy father."

He trembled ! she had raised her head
And asked " Where am I ? " " Here with me,"
He answered, " I will rescue thee ! "
The rich blood rushes through her veins
And blushes come, as still he clasps
Her to his heart.   And then his ear
Caught once again the Spanish cheer :

She seemed to him a feather then,
And he to her, strongest of men;
Speed now, good steed! thy footsteps fleet
May once again make safe retreat.

The bridge is passed—the moat is crost
The tall Knight's plume to sight is lost.
His horse's hoofs deep-print the sand,
He turns him thrice with clenched hand
And dares the fierce and ruthless foe
Who follow, but in vain pursue.

They reach the ship—but one—the last
Of all their matchless fleet remains;
They hoist upon its topmost mast
A standard, free from all such stains
As massacre hath this day given
To Spain's proud flag—" They cry to heaven!
The souls of these our martyred slain
Thus slaughtered, will they cry in vain?"

Thus thought the few who reached the ship;
For helpless ones in wakeless sleep
Were left unburied! With feast and song,
The Spanish victors boast this wrong;
For " might makes right," 'tis stoutly claimed
When Christian standards are unfurled

To drive the Moslem from the world!
To God the one for victory kneels,
To Allah the pious Turk appeals;
And each will pray, and fight, and die
Thinking that God, who rules the sky,
Will hear his prayer and damn his foe,—
And this is all we'll ever know
Of the God of Battles, for Mars
Hath not appeared since ancient wars.

※　　　※　　　※　　　※　　　※　　　*

THE FÊTE OF THE CONQUEROR.

Gay were the streets of Augustine
And thousands thronged to view the scene,
When Spanish chief, with crown of war,
Was seated like an Emperor,
      To while an idle hour.
The melodies of music sweet
Were wafted through the crowded street,
While courtiers hung around the feet
      Of this proud prince's power.

He smiled, and often waved his hand
To those who passed the Ducal stand,
Just as a king who ruled the land
      Would smile with haughty grace;

He bowed before the vulgar herd
And spoke the long-considered word,
To please the fawning, eager crowd
        Who view the ruler's face.

Anon he beckoned to a maid—
A dancer—who her devoirs paid
With sinuous and airy tread
        Which showed the hidden charm:
The little foot and ankle round,
The tapering limbs, so lightly gowned,
And then, at castanet's quick sound,
        The bare and lovely arm.

For now he wears the signet ring
Of haughty Spain's ascetic king,
And titled heralds loudly do cry:
        " Long live our noble Prince!
Menendez de Aviles, Knight
Of Calatrava; Prince by right
Of conquest, won by deeds of might;
And Duke of Augustine!

"Great chieftain of old Aragon!
A hundred fields in battle won
Proclaim him now Spain's greatest son
        And crown with laurel wreath:

Behold his gallant, martial brow
All seamed across by battle scar;
His foemen tremble from afar,
   Though sword be in its sheath!

"—Not one of all the Knights of Spain
Can show a crest as free from stain,
As his, whose valiant sword has slain
   A host of gallant foes;
Long live the bravest Knight of Spain!
Who hosts of heretics has slain;
Long live the Prince of proud Biscayne,
   And death to all his foes!"

A thousand *vivas* rent the air
When herald ceased. Then standards wave
And all the troops assembled there
Echo the shout: "Long live the brave!"

Ah! then was seen on summer night
Fit charms to tempt an anchorite!
The look of love from darkest eyes,
And *naïve* glance as maiden sighs;
The olive skin of clear brunette
And charms that tempt the bright lorgnette
At opera or festive ball,
And all our senses do enthrall!

To sounds of clicking castanet
Fair maidens danced the minuet,
With feet so small and limbs so round
That seeing seemed to silence sound;
With figures plump, handsome and light
And eyes that flashed 'neath hair of night,
Thus did these fair Minorcans dance,
With arms upturned of beauty rare
And footsteps light as zephyrs are!
Thus did the gay señor and maiden
Rejoice as if this land were Eden.

For now the great fête-day is here
And rattling drums and gleaming spear
And hosts of troops, both horse and foot,
The Adelantado salute.
The morrow dawns; at early noon,
Despite the rays of lurid sun
Which blaze with Southern noon-day heat,
Caballeros señoras greet,
At the *Plaza de Toros*,
The Bull, emerging from the keep
Where cruel fast had banished sleep,
And where the dungeon day seemed night,
And blinded by the dazzling light—
Now sees at last yon knight and steed
And charges both with tempest speed.

Mid *vivas* round the *plaza* noised
The knight rides forth ; his lance is poised,
His plume bends low toward the Duke,
With hand as firm and eye as clear
As ever graced a cavalier,
Or gave to plebe Patrician look.
As leaps the lion on its prey
So rushed the maddened bull that day ;
So plunged his horns within the breast
And sides of the defenceless beast
Which rears impaled, until at last
It falls, the life-blood flowing fast !

The Picador now leaps forth free
And turns, that all the crowd may see
How fearless is his gallantry ;
He turns again—and well he may—
For now the bull charges to slay,
And yet again ! and bears as prize
The blanket, which now veils his eyes ;
He bellows loud and, pausing, gores
The earth with rage ; in tatters tears
The blanket—then surveys the corse,
Shakes his head and sees—another horse !

The Picador now lies beneath
The dying steed, gasping for breath ;

Now man and horse are dragged away
Amid loud cries and music gay!
"Viva! Viva!" the people cry,
"Sevilla's champion draws nigh!"
Clad like the rest in colors gay
And flowing sash, careless as they—
While Matadores prick again
The maddened bull, which writhes with pain—
He scarcely deigns to notice how
Bold Toro looks—with graceful bow
He turns—just in the nick of time!
To 'scape the bull.

What recks the wounds on neck and breast?
"Caramba! what a gallant beast!
Let Carlos come!" Thus is the cry
Which sees the brave Pedrillo die!
While children and fair maidens feast
Their eyes upon the bloody beast
And dying man, with strange delight.
Yet Christians say this sport is right,
And children shout: Bravo, Toro!
And maidens laugh, and roses throw.

"Let Carlos come!" and at the word—
With blanket-shield and naked sword;
With whip-cord muscles, and graces

Fit to adorn great Hercules—
Leaped quick into the dread *Arene*
The champion of Augustine.

The " conqueror " looked on, meanwhile,
With pride of mien and gracious smile ;
And maids and dames of Augustine,
In gay attire, enjoyed the scene ;
For he, the conqueror, had come
To grant them *fêtes*, and knell the doom
Of other men as brave as these,
And murder maidens on bended knees !

The bull, half-blinded now with blood
And weakening fast, tottering stood
Defiant of the *vivas* loud,
Defiant of the heartless crowd ;
Until, at sound of bugle blast,
He charged again, and bore as crest
The crimson blanket.　Enraged anew
He three times charged, until he grew
Too weak to fight ; and then a stroke,
So truly dealt, that it did look
Like needle prick, ended the fight
And lifeless bull lay prone in sight ;
And joyous crowds cried loud again :
" Long live the Duke of Augustine ! "

They call this sport! themselves they call
The only Christians among us all!
This "arena:" like that of old
When Christian slaves were bought and sold
To furnish sport for Nero's eye,
Who laughed to see his victims die!

Not mad bull then, but tigers wild
And savage lions dared the field;
Not gold the object, but the life
Of Christian slaves hung on the strife!
There Princes said, as Pagans smiled:
" These be but Christians who are killed:
The babe which yonder tiger fed
Was taken from a Christian's bed!"
And, like to these, Menendez slew
As carelessly a Christian crew,
Who were "but Huguenots," 'tis true.

And who can say what error is,
When people claim that heresies
Blind those who will not tamely heed
Some special faith, or rite, or creed
The Chinese hold that only they,
Led by Confucius, know the way;
Four hundred million there do live
And yet, 'tis said, the records give,

With forty million Christians here,
More murders in a single year!

*　　*　　*　　*　　*　　*

With tireless wings the sea-gull flies
Greeting the breakers with its cries,
Nor rests, though turn him where he may
He views but billows of the sea;
Bird of the ocean! wing thy flight
Above the trackless waves to-night;
Peer down into the caverns deep
Where monsters in sea-valleys sleep,
For thou alone art monarch where
No other bird can soar in air;

Nor can the tempest's driving spray
Lashing the ocean, stem thy way;
Though clouds grew black as waves grew white,
While ebon folds of darkest night
Hung o'er the waters—obscured the shore
Until its lines were seen no more,—
The white gulls screamed, and skimmed the sea.
So strong of wing, so proudly free,
It seemed that they could ever flee!

The sea was rough and turbid waves
Arose on high, then yawned like graves

Or hollow troughs, wherein the blue
Beneath white crests was lost to view.
Ah, soul of love! uphold thy right,
For never did more sombre night
Cast shadows darker round a life
More fit to love, more cursed with strife!
Alas! on ocean's briny tracks
Were scattered fragments of the wrecks.

The Spanish chieftain scans the sky
Where dark clouds roll, where eagles fly
And swoop and dart cross lightning's path
And shriek with joy at tempest's wrath.
The day grows drear; dark clouds enfold
The opaque sky: then thunder rolled
With threatening sound, and blast on blast
'Neath heaven's dome succeeded fast,
And forked lightning traced the sky
With line of fire, dazzling the eye.

With form erect and steady pace
Menendez walked: his swarthy face
Frown'd sternly, while two thousand braves
Worked on the wall like galley slaves.

The Indian hath a soul as true
To love and hope, as if he drew

His life-blood from the whitest breast
That ever innocent caressed;
But now, condemned to labor there
And sleep at night in prison air,
His downcast look and humble mien,—
So unlike what he once had been—
Seemed rather that of conquered slave
Than free-born, fearless Indian brave.
So seemed one who, with head bent low,
Thus spake to the Adelantado:
"—Some Christians, wrecked on yonder shore,
Who seem to be in great distress,
Are making signals for succor."

'Twas in a wild, unsheltered spot
Where isles and islets check the sea,
And winds and waves play with the spray,
And salt-sea meadows seem to float:
'Twas where the luscious wild grapes hung
Profusely, from the vines low flung
That sweep the river's rising tides:
Where pomegranates, red-ripe and sweet,
Wave from the boughs and gently meet;
'Twas where the Indian's canoe glides,
That Spaniards stood along the shore
In battle-line, while 'cross the stream
Grouped close, were shipwrecked men, who bore

Standards and arms; and then the gleam
Of helmets, breast-plates, swords and shields,
Shone in the dazzling noon-day light;
And then—the sign that foeman yields —
They raised the flag of truce, all white.
Not there do lofty mountains stand
With crags and battlements in air,
But one long beach of whitest sand,
Fringes the wide blue waters there.
The loon and paroquet are seen,
And pelican and long-billed crane;
The " Lady of Waters " sails in sight
With graceful form, and plumage white;
And flocks of herons greet the wise curlew
Skimming the surface of the blue.

The Spaniards saw a gray-haired man,
Whose form was robust, tall, and lithe,
And round him crowded shipwrecked men
Who seemed to hold but lightly life,
If he would lead them in the strife;
But no! the chieftain bent his head
And kissed, with rev'rent courtesy,
The hand of Léonore.—" For thee,
Sweet lady, I would shackles wear
If that would save to thee a tear,—
If that would win thee from despair.

He turned toward the soldiers then :
"—And ye, my comrades, show yon men
The Huguenots' fidelity!"
Like vassals each bent loyal knee
Before the girl, that all might see
That which they held more sacred than
The proudest heritage of man :
Their knightly pledge of chivalry.
There knelt De Rohan, of noble line,
Whose fame was known from "Father Rhine"
To Pyrenees, and throughout Spain ;
De Gourgues, whose fame was far and wide,
Knelt by the Duke de Rohan's side ;
And other knights as brave as they
Knelt on the island beach that day.
By this one act, these gallant men
Brought back her former life again,
When all that rank and wealth confers,
Land, titles, honors, *all* were hers!

Now cresting waves, now lost to view,
Laudonnière guides the swift canoe
To where the swarthy Spaniards stand ;
But, ere he steps upon the land,
He waves them back with haughty hand,
Unbuckles belt, unsheathes his sword
And flings it far into the sea!

Then quickly drops upon one knee
To kiss again the maiden's hand,
Then leads her, like a queen, to land.
The Spaniards see the sword sink deep
Into the sea, but silence keep.

The signet of a woman's worth,
And surest test of gentle birth,
Is modesty,
The charm that links her to the sky,
The blossom that can never die!
They saw it when she veiled her face
As best she could, nor saw a trace
Of all the deep, unspoken woe
Which noble natures will not show.
And when the eager Spaniards saw
Her modest mien they looked with awe
Upon such patience as she then,
In presence of these hostile men,
Thus sweetly showed.   Though veiled her face,
They could but note her faultless grace :
The gentleness, yet princely air
With which she met their glances there.

With form erect and noble head,
Like one whose place it was to lead,
The chieftain to Menendez said :

"—I've come to ask a soldier's aid—
Not for myself—'twere idle here
To seek to save Laudonnière—
But as a soldier I do crave
The lives of yonder soldiers brave.
My silver hairs have done with strife,
And soon as thou hast said, the life
Of lady Léonore shall be
As pure, as sacred, and as free
As when a ruthless king exiled
The Admiral Coligny's child ;
And promise me that thou wilt spare
The lives of men who famish there,
Yet who most willingly will die
With arms in hand, rather than try
A captive's fate : Chieftain, I swear
Their penalty and mine to bear.
I yield—do what thou wilt with me,
But aid the rest to cross the sea."

"—Thou pleadest as the brave do plead,
Who only do the noble deed ;
I do not war upon the fair,
The maiden hath no cause for fear,
Nor have thy men, for I will spare
The lives of all who yield them here.
As for Coligny's child, I swear,

Even were she of the Moslem sect,
Menendez would *her* life protect."

The veteran started at this name,
And said, with eyes kindling aflame :
"—Then thou art he who twice hath dared
To cope with me—whom I have spared
E'en when thy form was 'neath my knee!
Then maidens sought in vain to flee ;
Then was my heel upon thy neck,
And round us lay, in mortal wreck,
Defenceless men and women, slain
By thy command, false knight of Spain!
Now hear me! though shipwrecked and few,
And though my men thy host doth view,
And though we do not yield to thee,
But rather to the stormy sea :—
I curse thee, Spaniard, to thy face
For that inhuman, vile disgrace!"

Menendez' face grew angry black,
As haughtily he waved him back
And muttered :—"Thou shalt feel the rack!"

Where fair Nature smiled with Spring's sweetest
    smile
The Huguenots landed, on the shores of an Isle
Where a herd of wild deer freely browsed 'neath the
    trees,
Till a high-antlered stag raised his head, snuffed the
    breeze,
And, with one warning note, led the fear-stricken
    troop,
With a fleet, airy leap swiftly past the strange group
Through the wild orange grove till they passed out
    of sight.
And an old Indian stood watching them, and the
    flight
Of the fast fleeing deer; then he held up an oar,
And beckoned the strangers to come from the shore.
His countenance was grave and his long raven hair
Proclaimed him a Prophet.   With a wish to beguile
The slow hours away while at rest in this bay
They had come to the shore on this bright summer
    day;
But when the old Indian by signs told the tale
Of the late massacre,—swarthy faces turned pale,
For they saw their comrades had been massacred
    there !

When he showed them, by signs, how these Hugue-
    nots fell—

How the bones of the dead, left to bleach on yon
  hill,
Were the sport of coyotes, and the carrion prey
Of yon vultures that hovered over them and the
  sea,—
And showed them the hollows made by claws in the
  sands
Whence the flesh had been torn from the manacled
  hands
Of the unburied slain;—the waves witnessed then,
As they close-clenched their hands, the oaths of
  these men!

"—Speed, vengeance! thou art mine, fierce child of
  my love!
Hear my oath, and record it, ye angels above!
I swear by high heaven to give blood back for blood,
Take an eye for an eye, render Cæsar his due,
And hang high as Haman these men, who have shed
The blood of the helpless!
Ah! can it be true? shall I see thee no more,
Sweet angel? my idol, my own Léonore!"

Then his eyes caught the words deep engraved on a
  tree:
"—Not as Frenchmen, but Lutherans, that all men
  may see

The vengeance of Catholics, when foul heresy
Lifts its head in this land! I, the Adelantado
Pedro Menendez, for King Philip of Spain,
And for our Religion, have in Florida slain
Three hundred heretics,—all Frenchmen and Hu-
　　guenots!"

As the blast to the thunder, as the flash to the vein
Of red lightning, which rends the black heavens in
　　twain,
The fierce indignation of Count Ribault broke forth
As he held high his hand and then uttered an oath,
With heaven as witness, and the manes of the dead
And the waves of the sea to hear what he said.
"All Frenchmen and traitors!"—then flashed on
　　his brain
The hopeful reflection: "Léonore was not slain,
And I'll search the wide earth till I find her again!"
　　*　　　*　　　*　　　*　　　*　　　*

Finer than fabrics from the loom　　　　　　·
Is that which spiders weave in tomb
Of human captives—a web so fine,
So intricate its silken meshes,
And soft as maiden's lovely tresses,
That Solomon could scarce divine
Its mystery of warp and woof

As spider spun on dungeon roof;
Nor human hands, with all the skill
Which art subjects to human will,
Toiling labor from morn to night,
Can fashion fabrics so frail and slight
Yet strong enough for spider's weight.
It twines its net where struggling fly
And ruthless spider drawing nigh,
Greet the captive's eye. The ball
From which the spinner spun this thread
Seemed small but limitless, and made
So as to let the spider fall
Or climb it with as steady air
As if the skeins formed winding stair.
The spider claimed him as a friend
And crawled unharmed upon his hand.
Oft in the vigils of the night
Minutes seemed hours, and Time's slow flight
Pictured the hollowness of fame
Which had so trumpeted his name:
Why was he now, whose former power
Could summon round him in an hour
A thousand men who followed where
His black plume led—whose single sword
Was worth a thousand more—ignored
By friends and foes alike!
Thus were the captive's thoughts, for he
Knew nothing of the treachery

Which had given his comrades o'er
To massacre; nor that Léonore
Was now a captive.   He thought that she
Had, long ere this, reached France and home,
And that the maiden's life was free
Because of his selected doom.
"—Hard as it is," the captive said,
" 'Tis sweet to know I saved the maid; that I
Alone, in felon's cell shall die."

He could not raise his form upright,
So short the chain—so bent his form
With failing strength: and though the light
Of day brightened with joyous gleam
The world without, 'twas dark as night
Within the cell where the captive lay,
Who scarce could tell the night from day.

He bent his head:—" 'Twas but the sea
Beating with sad monotony
My prison walls.   No voice comes nigh,
No living thing, no laugh, nor sigh,
No fellowship, nor sympathy
Of human-kind e'er comes to me!
What now am I ? 'tis useless here—
'Tis worse than useless anywhere—
To prate of ills that captives bear.

I'll welcome death most willingly,
But, long as fate confines me here,
It shall not humble Laudonnière!
As strong in will, though weak in frame,
As careful of my own good name,
As resolute as if proud fame
With trumpet notes and loud acclaim
Pronounced me great :—come woe, come weal,
They'll find my mettle truest steel!"

He scarce had finished, when the sound
Of stealthy steps entered his cell;
He raised him from the damp, cold ground
And bent his head to listen well:
"—Speak, friend! who greets Laudonnière,
What human soul approaches near?"
'Twas dark as midnight—though evening sun
In cirrous skies had scarce begun
To course toward its setting. A light
Struck by an Indian, flint to flint—
As miner's strokes in caverns glint—
Revealed to the old captive's sight
An Indian brave, who sought to flee—
For wrists and ankles showed that he
Had borne but lately clanking chains
That left upon his limbs their stains.—
With hand on lip as if to say:

"—Keep silence, captive, that I may
Make good escape;"—he raised a stone,
Waved quick farewell, leaped down, was gone!
The fugitive had left no trace
And, as the stone dropped back in place,
The captive smiled:—"One prisoner less,
One thought the more, one hope to bless
And cheer at last my loneliness—"

What more the captive might have said
We do not know; another tread
He heard—a step that often ceased,
The cat-like footstep of a priest—
For only he did sometimes come
To wrest the captive from the tomb:
And often had he tried—and failed—
To change a heart that never quailed.
He answered thus the scheming priest:
"—Not for the charms of liberty,
Not for my life, will I to thee,
False priest, forswear the past, forswear
The principles that cast me here.
My honor as a man is given
To hold me true—'fore man and heaven—
And not for all the sweets of peace
Would I thus purchase my release.
Go! caitiff, go! and tell thy master

My strength may fail, my sores may fester,
And life, receding, bend my frame,
Yet I will not recant, or shame
That which I prize the most—my name!"

The bolts were drawn, a priest came in
With shuffling gait and subtle mien,
And, as the captive turned his head,
The crafty Spaniard softly said:
"—Laudonnière, a slave hath fled—
Thy freedom I will grant to thee
If thou wilt shew this slave to me,—
A crazy girl escaped to-day
From her chamber—came she this way?
I fear me 'twas her artful hand
Which did unlock the iron band
That bound the Guale chieftain's wrist,
And freed the captive from the priest."

"—Not mine the task, nor mine the will,
To act the spy, or secrets tell;
I would far rather aid the flight
Of captive, be he red or white,
Than show thee, like a sleuth-hound, where
Slaves flee from masters in despair!
Go ask thy victims! Question the dead,
And let them say where he hath fled!"

The cell door opened, the man of blood,
Menendez, in the doorway stood;
No pity was in that dark face
For him who would not sue for grace.
All, all was dark, cruel and cold;
Base spirit in a breast so bold,
That none but stoutest knight could stand
Before the weight of his strong brand.

The face of old Laudonnière
Evinced no change; no trace of fear,
No thought nor look, nor tinge of shame
Across that manly visage came.
He raised his feeble form as high
As chains and pillar would allow,
And looked to see who thus drew nigh,
But did not deign to speak or bow.
The man whom he had spared was there
To gloat upon his proud despair!
The scornful glance shone in his eye
Turned full upon Menendez then,—
The knowledge that he soon must die
Or yield, but stronger nerved the man;
The long white hair fell down his back,
The long white beard concealed his neck,
And tattered garments clothed the wreck
Of stout and bold Laudonnière;

But still he would not breathe a prayer.
"—Thou art the last—ill-fated man—
The very last of all thy clan
Save one—the lady Léonore.
If thou art stubborn, obdurate,
She shall endure as hard a fate
As withered flower;—Léonore
Shall, after pleasure's reign is o'er,
Speak humbly, yield unto my will
Long after thy cold corse is still!

Like thee, she is defiant now;
Like thine, her spirit will not bow;
I swear that she shall know my rage
Like 'prisoned bird in gilded cage;
Know what it is to make a foe
Who still is loath to strike the blow
Fatal to hope, which virtue rends
And leaves her to the scorn of friends!
No other hope, no other aid
Is thine, but thou canst save the maid
And thy poor life, if thou wilt say
' I am a Catholic,' this day."

Then flashed the captive's eyes with ire:
"—If death await—and death by fire—
I hold myself, ruffian, too true

To falsely kneel, or basely sue!
My shrunken limbs are well-nigh bare;
My form is bent, and white my hair;
But, Spaniard, hear!   I would not crave
One boon fron· thee my life to save!
Rather than live a life of shame
I'd welcome the red tongue of flame;
Feel the knout, or suffer my back
To be slow-broken by yon rack.
But Léonore!"—One arm was raised
And voice grew hoarse as eyes now blazed—
One shackle snapped—one hand was free,
And, quick as thought, one giant blow
From angry captive felled his foe!

    *   *   *   *   *   *

What does she there?   Yon maiden fair
As is the fresh young budding rose,
Looks down with sweet abstracted air
Where soft and full Matanzas flows:
Where sun-light ripples, dancing, gleam,
And willows, stooping, kiss the stream.
She sees it all; and thinks that she,
Hidden by curtain drapery,
Herself is all unseen: and yet
The curtain, nor the falling hair
Nor dress, conceal a budding pair
Which peeps from out the summer fold

And shows the charm of youth, untold,
Unknown, and pure as vestal vase
Or as the gentle maiden's face;
So pure, so fair and innocent,
So young and lovely, that 'twas meant,
Undoubtedly, to grace a home:
This flower budding into bloom.

And who is she? who leans now o'er
The balcony to pluck a flower
From creeping vine, which clambers there
To mingle flowers with her hair?
Thus thought a minstrel who drew near
And tuned the strings of soft guitar;
She looks and sighs as mem'ry brings
Its treasure store—the minstrel sings:

" *The moving clouds with mantle gray*
Float peacefully, onward, away;
And 'neath thy surface, flashing bright,
Gleam stars like diamonds of the night:
Flow, rio, flow! away! away!
Haste onward to the rolling sea!

" *Behold the sheen from fleecy fold*
Flash in the stream, like wan of gold,
And, 'joy the moonbeams dancing quiver

Gilding the wavelets of the river ;
Roll onward to the deep blue sea,
Flow, rio, flow ! away ! away !

" The earth is covered o'er with green
And moon-lit sky is soft, serene
Where countless stars with silv'ry light
Kindle the pathless dome of night ;
Flow, rio, flow ! away ! away !
Mingle thy currents with the sea.

" The great Magnolia's flowers glow
To-night like lilies, white as snow ;
The breeze is sweet with perfumes rare
That ladens this soft Southern air ;
Would, would that she with me could view
Thy dimpled stream, rio, adieu ! "

Why starts from eyes the pearly tear?
Why shudders she with sudden fear?
Is it because the maiden's glance
Hath seen a form she knew in France?
Is it for this the maiden kneels
And clasps her hands in silent prayer?
He knows not that the maiden kneels
But quick attunes his sweet guitar;
While sentry's step goes back and forth

From north to south, from south to north,
And sentry's cry of: "All is well!"
Is answered from yon castle-wall;
And, scarcely had the red thrush bade
His sweet adieu in the neighb'ring glade,
When the minstrel sang this serenade:

" I come from a land afar, a land where soft guitar
    And the magic flute,
Reply to harper's strain, reply with love's refrain
    Reply—with sweet salute.

" Bright stars of tropic sky, full moon slow sailing by
    On peaceful azure sea ;
Aid now the minstrel's lay, where is my lady—say—
   Oh ! stars tell this to me !

Dear eyes of deepest blue ; dear heart so proudly true,
    Sweet little lily hand !
Would I could clasp again, form, hand, and heart in
  mine,
    Then life might gladly end !

Where does my lady sleep ? may angels vigils keep
    Over my lady's rest ;
Sweet be her slumbers deep, may no dark troubles sweep
    Over my lady's breast !

I've crossed the stormy sea, dear love, in search of thee,
　　Come, love! hasten to me;
Here 'neath the orange tree, lady I'll wait for thee,
　　Hasten, my love, to me!

As minstrel ceased, a paper scroll
From prison window was let fall.
He seized it, bore it to his lips,
Then hearkened to the sentry's step.
"—Gain quickly, minstrel,"—thus it read,
" Gain quickly yonder chaparral. . . . ."
And then he heard the hurried tread
Of many feet in castle hall :—
"—You stand as if upon the brink
Of some hot crater ;—blood—not ink
Serves now my pen ;—flee, Ribault, flee! ꜱ
If, unknown minstrel, thou art he!"
The clash of arms, the cries of men,
As minstrel fled, resounded then.

Ah fatal beauty! thine the store
Whence come thy troubles, Léonore!
Not Lethe's bliss, but chalice full
Of misery, alas! is thine!
For he too, knelt at beauty's shrine—
The Spanish chief—who saw the charm
Of pensive face and graceful form,

Which gave to thee that beauty rare.
Which doomed thy heart to mute despair!

'Twas when he whiled an idle hour
In her sweet presence, one balmy day,
He felt the mute unconscious power
Of innocence; nor dared to say
One ruffian word. Her gentleness,
Her saddened eyes and dire distress,
Forbade an act, or e'en a word
Which purity could not have heard
Without a blush. Though prisoned·here
Her every want was well supplied
As if she were the chieftain's bride;
Nor did she know that Laudonnière
Was chained a prisoner: nor that those
Who had surrendered to their foes
Without a blow, had all been slain;
She only wondered why this chief,
Who seemed to share a captive's grief,
Could prison her, to whom he swore
He'd share his love, and pledge his life,
If she would only be his wife.

Who knows right well the human breast
Knows that such love, when gently drest,
Uttered alike with voice and eye

And manner of deep sympathy,
Doth nurture love, or gratitude
Where love is not : hence 'twas she stood
Before Menendez—not as a foe
Nor as a captive, but as one
Who sought to soften the harsh blow
Of unrequited love.—" Señor, why
Am I kept in captivity?
What is my crime? why this duress?
Can one who loves me thus oppress
Her whom he asks to share his life!
To yield her love to him as wife?
And where is he—Laudonnière—
Best and bravest ! my noblest friend,
Who yielded to thy conquering hand?"

" My king, sweet lady, with harsh command
Forbids our union.   I kiss thy hand
And swear—despite my loyal oath—
If Catholic with Huguenot
Shall wed, to make thee mine, as soon
As thou shalt grant the priceless boon,
Thy willing hand.   Throughout this land
From North to South, from sand to sand
Of either sea, I rule alone—
All—all I have shall be thine own :
Then cast thy foolish faith aside,
And thou shalt be a ruler's bride.

And, Léonore, I swear to thee
A husband's faithful loyalty.
This fortress-castle, San Marco
Shall be thine own ; and lives no foe
So void of sense, so bold of tongue
Who ever hath the gauntlet flung,
Before the Adelantado,
Who hath not quailed beneath my blow !
Thou a prisoner now, can be
The mistress of this land and sea ;
And reign as mistress in a heart
Which hath not known thy counterpart :
Which hath not learned to love before,
But yields now captive—Léonore!"

Menendez paused—but no reply
Greeted the ardent lover's eye,
'Twas then they heard, from orange grove
The minstrel's song ; and low and sweet
From yonder tree a cooing dove
Began its lay. He strode away,
Like captain who has lost the day,
And sought the garden, where the breeze
From ocean cooled his brow, and trees
Seemed beckoning to him to come
And listen to the song. His gloom
Was changed to wrath : Who is he

Who comes, as to a trysting tree,
And sings, as if 'twas Léonore
Not minstrelsy, which brings him here?"

Menendez rose—not then did wire
Belt the wide earth with electric fire,
Nor 'cross the valleys of the sea,
Flash lightning currents: so rapidly
That what was done, but yesterday,
Is known to all the world to-day.
Nor had he heard how France had freed
All Huguenots; nor that the deed,
Which whelmed in one three hundred graves,
Was known to Ribault and his braves—
Whelmed in one? we erred, for not one
Was made when that dark deed was done!

Impatient frowns furrowed his face
As Menendez watched the minstrel's place;
—"Who is he?" thus the chieftain thought
Yet listened—not to music's note,
But to the words—"Yon minstrel's air
Is not such as Bohemians bear;
Nor yet is he like Troubadour;
No licensed minstrel he, I swear!
'Tis some dare-devil lurking here!
Methought all were slain—Moscoso

Shall suffer should he prove a foe!"
And then Menendez saw the scroll,—
The maiden's anxious look:—and all
The fears of doubting lover's soul
Began the chieftain to appal;
Nor was he last among the men
Who fast pursued the minstrel then.

A vase of flowers cast fragrance o'er
The prison room, as Léonore,—
Who saw the minstrel scale the wall
And heard the sentry's challenge call,
And saw pursuers fast pursue
And heard still others cry and hue—
Knelt tremblingly to pray.

Fair as the rose in early bloom
Was she who entered then the room;
Pure as the lily seemed her face
Where innocence, and love, and grace
Had gently stamped their sweet impress:
And yet she wore the convent's dress:
The synonym of gentleness.

The Nun's quick footsteps softly glide
Close to the kneeling captive's side;

A light hand on her shoulder fell,
And then she heard a figure kneel,
And saw the "sister's" spotless veil.

One saw a Protestant's sweet face,
One felt a Catholic's embrace,
And when, their silent prayers o'er,
The sweet young Nun led Léonore,
She went with her, hand clasped in hand,
As if she was some long-loved friend.

Trust forms its own sweet alchemy,
And welds our hearts with sympathy ;
And though as strangers met these two,
Each felt that new-found friend was true.
The stranger led her to the door,
Then through the hall, and Léonore
With trusting heart, and yielding hand
And earnest look, followed her friend :
She knew not who she was, nor cared,
She only knew that each had dared
To brave the Spanish chieftain's ire,
Born of a libertine's desire.

They quickly traversed then the hall,
Entered the garden, stood at the wall,—
And then the Spanish maiden said '

In Spanish tongue :—" Yon dark gray mass,
Is a Convent, and if, alas!
Menendez hath cast eyes on thee,
'Twere better that the grave should be
Thy heart's refuge! tears turn to stone
When virtue yields ; thy hope alone
Sweet friend is yonder Convent, where
No human might can harm a hair
Of thy young head.   Thy friends are slain ;
But one now lives : Laudonnière,
Who suffers in a gloomy cell,
And suffers more than mortal pain.
Persuade thyself to enter there—
No safety dwells for thee elsewhere."
The two embraced, and then the Nun
Left Léonore to pray alone ;
For none but willing heart could wear
The sacred veil of vestal there ;
For they are pure, and ev'ry race
Hath need to bless the " Sister's " face,
Which is as gentle, and as chaste
As chaste can be in human breast.

With outstretched arms in pleading prayer
The stricken girl stood trembling there,
A victim to her dark despair!
The future seemed a dread abyss

And life full of unhappiness;
She heeded not the threatening sky
Or whistling wind swift passing by;
The rain swept o'er her, and the storm
Seemed reaching down to seize her form,
And yet she stood by open gate
And thought of the poor minstrel's fate,
A victim to the Spaniard's hate!
And then of all those gallant men
By treachery, in cold blood slain;
She heard again the battle cries:
The shriek of her who vainly flies;
The maid's appeal; the wild despair
When children's brains are dashed in air,
And stricken mothers welter there!

She did not know, 'till now, 'twas he
Who caused this wanton butchery.
Despite the storm the captive stands
And raises up beseeching hands
In earnest, heartfelt prayer:

"—*Father in heaven, Creator of light*
Guide, in the darkness, my footsteps to-night,
Protect me from despair;
Alone and friendless I pray in thy sight
Heavenly Father! shield me with Thy might,
Heed an orphan's prayer! '

Christ my Redeemer, my trust is in Thee,
Life is a burdensome trial to me,
  Let me Thy refuge share;
Last of my race, I pray unto Thee
Jesus, my Saviour! let death set me free,
  Heed an exile's prayer!"

A heavy hand her two hands grasped,
An arm around her waist was clasped,
She struggled, then, her hands to free
And, struggling, sank upon her knee;
He raised her gently, then released
The maiden, whom he thus addressed:

—"Thy fears, sweet lady, are misplaced,
I'd have them by full trust replaced;
I would not harm thee, gentle maid,
For all the realms God ever made!
But thou shouldst know that, though thou art
A captive here, and though my heart
Gives all its wealth of love to thee,
Yet thou canst never hope to flee.

"More watchful than the lynx's eyes
Are eyes of love, which quick descries
Each longing of thy heart to leave
Him who would be thy willing slave,

List to me well: I love thee more,
Sweet, peerless, lovely Léonore
Than I have ever loved before;
Mine is not passion's fleet desire,
That fans to flame to soon expire—
A Spaniard loves with fiercer fire—
It rests with thee to end this strife,
And sweeten every hour of life
By bidding my fond hopes to live:
I'll give thee all that love can give—
Wealth, honors, power, and a place
Well suited to thy queenly grace."

Like one unnerved by startling fear,
She followed up the castle stair;
She answered not, nor sought to check
The sudden tears, for now the wreck
Of new-born hopes had sadly fled;
Nor did it seem that she had heard
Of all his speech a single word:—
And, waxing wroth, Menendez said:
"Choose quick! for maiden I do swear
"'Tis thus alone that thou can'st save
Thy saviour from a felon's grave;
Yield now to me thy willing hand,
Or I will give the harsh command
To swing from yonder turret high

Him, whom *thou* hast condemned to die!
Consent—and he shall go forth free
And thou shalt strike the shackles loose,
Refuse—and thy old friend shall die.
Shrink not from me! each shrieking cry
Within these walls will seem a sigh
This stormy night.   Nor pride of race
Shall free thee from my fond embrace,
Till hag grows haggard, dame beldame
And all my troops shall mock thy shame ! "

Then spake the Nun, who at the door
Stood unperceived by Léonore :
—" Forbear, Menendez, I forbid !
Think not that thy base crimes are hid !
'Tis not two years since Inez died ;
I saw thee tear the cloth aside
And gaze on thy victim—poor child !
Pure as a blossom undefiled ;
Sweet as the violet, and bright
As is the sunbeam to the sight.
Two years ago—and fair as truth ;
Inez died in the bloom of youth !
Deceived by thee, then cast aside
Ere thou hadst made her thy young bride ! "
The Nun then turned to Léonore :

—" Leave thou the world, its charity,
Though loud proclaimed by Pharisee,
Closes its doors, shuts out the light
From woman's heart with cruel might;
Leave thou the world, that turns its back,
Unlike the Christ, upon the wreck
Of innocence! Prosperity
With purple robes and livery
Scoffs at the poor; while poverty
Bears down yon crouching misery!
The guilty 'scape, the guiltless flee,
And man laughs on!

       The common herd
Lingers to hear each ribald word,
And all approve—for wealth was power
When he, a villain, ruled the hour
Two years ago with pleasures gay,
To while the summer days away;
Meanwhile she died—ruthlessly slain!"

She said no more. The fearful strain,
It seemed, had clouded now the brain
Of Léonore; with timid glance
She turned to meet the Nun's advance,
But when the last sad moment came
To save his life—whate'er the cost—

Her woman's heart o'ercame her pride,
And then she gave her hand as bride.
Again the Nun cried,—" I forbid!"
And Léonore, with swimming head
And reeling brain, sank to the floor;
The gentle Nun, now bending o'er
Her senseless form, chafed hands and face
And waved Menendez from the place.

She held him by some mystic power,
For, though Menendez would not cower
Before a mortal, yet he obeyed
Reluctantly, then, turning, said:
—" Nina, away! that mortal dies—
Be she like angel from the skies—
Who thwarts my will, or thus defies
Menendez here? Dost thou not know
That there are cells 'neath San Marco
Where e'en a Nun may chance to lie?"

—" I know it well, and thee defy!
Thou darest not doom me to die;
I saved thee once—ungrateful man
Away! or thou shalt feel the ban
From which my prayers once saved thee!"

Whate'er the cause, the chief obeyed ;
Whate'er the end, the Nun did lead
The lady Léonore away
Unhindered, ere the dawn of day ;
And once within those convent walls
No human might the will appals :
No power, save divine, can make
Unwilling bride a husband take ;
Nor will even Menendez dare
The wrath of her who governs there.

    *   *   *   *   *   *

Far sound the cries of swift curlew,
And slowly now a small canoe
All softly glided into view ;
The oar so lightly touched the stream
It seemed unreal—some fairy dream
Of Arcadie—and she a sprite
Who ruled the sylvan stream at night ;
Her shoulders and her arms were bare,
Her bronze-like breasts, a wondrous pair,
Though half-concealed by raven hair,
Seemed fairer, fuller, rounder far
Than those of Milo's Venus are.

She gained the centre of the stream
And watched the fast-descending gleam
Of sunset on the farther shore

As if to list the sound of oar
Or see another bateau glide
Toward her own, from yonder side.

The partridge from its covert fled,
The wild sea-crane raised high its head;
The plover, too, as quickly hied;
And loud the flying wild-goose cried;
As down the west the setting sun
Tinted the brilliant horizon
With glowing light; at last its ray
Kisses the hills, then fades away:
The amber light now fills the vales
With soft re-glow, then slowly trails
The deepening shadows of twilight
Until the earth is veiled by night.
A maiden grieves, as lovers grieve—
For Indian loves as others love—
Her eyes, which looked with fond love-light
To Coacoochee's eyes last night
Now weep with premonition's woe,
As the hours, fleeting, come and go
And he comes not. At trysting place,
With beating heart and anxious face,
She lingers long and patient waits,
Prays to the Sun—and all the Fates
That Coacoochee may be spared:

For well she knows that he hath dared
To grapple with the Spanish foe.

With the great Adelantado
Whose iron heart and arm of might
She knew the chief would seek in fight.
She trembled then—for who that loves
As did this maiden, hath not fears
When such a foe as this appears?
Perchance her own fond lover may
Fall 'neath this doughty chieftain's knee--
For well she knew he would not flee—
She knew that he would fighting, fall,
Or sound the Spanish chieftain's knell
With homeward thrust and Indian yell;
'Till foeman welters in his gore,
And Spaniard falls to rise no more!
For thus the Indian chieftain swore:
—" My Thronatiska ere the sun
Shall rise, and sink 'neath horizon,
The wrongs, oppressions, and disgrace
Which hath so manacled my race—
Until the once free Seminole
Hath supple knee and coward soul,—
Shall be revenged! Our foes shall die
Ere sun hath reddened Western sky!

—" But Thronatiska, sweet—my own!—
In life, in death, we are but one;
Thy dark-brown eye, like the gazelle's,
Is full of tears; thy bosom swells,
And trembling form clasped close to mine
Says thou art mine, as I am thine!
Farewell! should I not hither come—
To kiss these cheeks like rose a-bloom—
Thou'll meet me in the spirit home."

   *   *   *   *   *   *

Eyes that were radiant, why are they sad?
Sweet Thronatiska what hast thou read
In the pages of evening till the sun-tints were gone,
Hands clasped above thee, pleading alone?

Bride of the honey-moon where is thy bridegroom?
Blossom of happiness where is thy bloom?
Heaves now her bosom, eyes scarce can see,
Hear her, Great Spirit, pleading to thee!

Heaves now her bosom, eyes scarce can see:
—" World that I loved so, farewell to thee!"
Sweet zephyrs of evening, murmur afar,
Murmur the sorrows of Thronatiska!

Pride of the Seminole, lovely brown thrush,
Slowly the sun-set deepens its blush;

Pure as the dew-drop, or pearl of the sea,
Pride of the Seminole, farewell to thee!

Waiting, still waiting, till the sun went to rest
Down the vales of the evening afar in the West:
—" Shroud of deep waters,—green grave of the sea,—
Soul of my lover! I hasten to thee!"

—" World that I loved so!" Earth, sea, and sky
Saw the brown bosom heave its last sigh!
Willows bent lower sadly to weep
When sweet Thronatiska sank in the deep!

Far down the river a batcau floats free,
On with the current and out to the sea,
While the white bubbles sadly show where
Sweet Thronátiska sank in despair!

Billows of the ocean, clasp your white hands,—
Wave touching wave,—till again the white sands
Receive as their own, while the waves dirge afar,
The form of the beautiful Thronatiska!

* * * * * *

Down 'neath the castle, up from the cells
Following stairways, filling the halls,
Sound now a-near the fierce Indian yells:
Sounding the din of a murderous war,
Coming now nearer, then going afar.

Clotted with gore an Indian chief—
Whose step was soft as falling leaf,
Whose eye was like an eagle's when
It sweeps from topmost crag to glen,
Fixes its talons on its prey
Then loudly screams and soars away—
Entered the hall where Ribault stood,—
His sword likewise red stained with blood,—
For, while the Indian maiden prayed,
And, though the combat was delayed,
Before the Spanish chief could seal
His triumph with a single kiss
Or rob the convent of its prize:
They heard the sudden, startling peal
Of cannon loud, and arquebuse,
'Mid clang of battle and fierce cries.

As victors now the Frenchmen cry;
Like heroes brave do Indians die,
And, foremost, Coacoochee stood
With savage hands red-dyed in blood.

The hall was filled—a score of men
With clashing arms approached him then.

The Adelantado was brave,
Whatever his great faults might be,
Let this be said : he would not save
His life, or theirs, by poltroonry ;
Nor would he seek to 'scape a foe
Till his stout arm had dealt a blow
That none, save skilful hands, could feel
And bear up 'neath his flashing steel.

Ribault advanced—waved back his men
Who yielded like a Scottish clan
To Scottish chief:—" I scorn," he said
" To summon others to my aid,
I scorn to basely fight a foe
Who cannot strike back blow for blow ;
I know right well thy crimes demand
A felon's death ; but here I stand
To fight thee with my single brand :
Draw, Spaniard, and thy life defend ! "

Menendez glared, with eyes of hate
Like bated bull defying fate,
—" I know thee well, but fear thee not

Thou caitiff, rebel Huguenot!
Methought De Guise had laid thee low
With arm of might and loyal blow.
I know thee well! thy cursed life
Hath been my goal in former strife,
And now, though hosts may heed thy call,
Here will I die 'gainst Spanish wall—
'Gainst thee Ribault—'gainst one and all!"

Now blade to blade, and hilt to hilt,
The combatants fought round the room,
And now the blood of one is spilt,
Which seems to knell Count Ribault's doom!
But that young chieftain heeds it not,
And Catholic and Huguenot
Crowd round the two, with eager look
Watching each parry and each stroke;
Now sinks Ribault upon one knee,
Then up, like lightning, and as free,
Though bleeding fast! The blades bright flashed
Until the Spaniard's sword was dashed
Across the hall and, though unharmed,
He stood before Ribault disarmed.
With sullen glare from eyes of hate
Menendez waited then his fate,
Nor sought to leave the fatal place,
Nor deigned to utter word of grace.

—" Now go!" cried Ribault, " thou art free
If thou dost pledge thy word to me
To lead thy troops beyond the sea!"
—" I promise," said the chief, " for they,
Though overcome this fatal day,
I know have fought most gallantly.
But for myself, Count Ribault, know
I am—shall ever be—thy foe!"

     *   *   *   *   *   *

The midnight air seemed sadly still :
Menendez walked the silent hill ;
His martial figure muffled close
Strode back and forth before a cross.
Anon he drew his watch, then scanned
The moonlit path and seemed unmanned ;
The strong man's frame like aspen shook
While earnest face with haggard look
Was fixed upon the tomb and grave
Of Inez—once his doting slave.

At last he knelt, with fevered head,
Before the tomb and humbly prayed ;
A touch as light as swaying leaf
Caressed his head now bowed with grief ;
A hand then rested gently there,
And then a woman knelt in prayer

Beside the man whose love had won
Her heart—and left her life undone!
That heart which once had quickly beat
When this proud chief knelt at her feet—
Which he had sweetly woo'd and won—
Was tranquil now. To him the Nun,
So near and yet so far from him,
Like a good angel then did seem,
While he thus bowed did seem to her
Like a forsaken wanderer!

The world was changed: the sufferer
With chastened grief was comforter,
While princely chief, bereft of power,
Before his victim seemed to cower;
And when that gentle face met his,
Menendez sank upon his knees
And bowed his head in grief:—" Nina,
My wronged angel! come fly with me,
I cannot leave this land and thee!"
'   The soft moonlight
Shone on a figure dressed in white:
The wind arose—and well it might—
To silence him when she, that night,
With one hand pointing to the tomb,
Stretched forth the other to the gloom
Which shrouded yonder convent wall

And closed from her the world and all!
He seized her hand, bent down to kiss
That lily hand which once was his!
Then groaned with anguish, for alone
He knelt beside the cross of stone.

The moon sailed forth, and stars slipped out
From 'hind the clouds, while round about
Him lay the graves—he saw but one—
The grave of her whose love he'd won
Then cast aside like wilted flower
Or plaything of an idle hour.
She whom he had refused to wed
Sank slowly till she died! The Nun,
Meanwhile, had left him there alone.

The clouds grew black; and dark as they
The old, old frown came back.—Away
The chang'd man strode, resolved to die
Or win again supremacy.
The cup was bitter! She refused;
Inez, whose love he had abused,
But whom he loved—was now no more;
And 'sdeath! the lady Léonore
Perchance would soon be Ribault's bride!

With muttered curse and rapid stride
And muffled form he neared the wood

Nor halted, 'till at last he stood
Amid his sleeping men : for they
Had taken oath to cross the sea.
He laid him down, but could not sleep :
A raging tempest seemed to sweep
Across his breast.   From castle height,
Where Ribault's standard waved in sight,
He heard the sentry's—" All is well ! "
Then rose again with clenchèd hand
And stood amid his sleeping band,
He strode him forth, now up, now down,
Along the lone and wide sea beach,
With hardened heart and angry frown
To list to what wild billows teach—
He looked above, the star-lit sky
Shone o'er the sea resplendently :
Ten million gems, whose diamond light
Twinkled as merrily that night
As if defeat had not a pall
Cast over hope, and life, and all !
He turned his eyes and viewed the sea
Far-reaching as yon azure dome :
—" Let thy deep waters hide from me
The tortures of a vassal's doom !
Aye, 'tis worse ! an exile, driven,
Like a poor hind, from this fair Eden
Where I have ruled supreme, alone
Obeyed and feared, as if the throne

Of Spain's empire was all my own!"
He smiled, this thought at least was sweet,
It passed as it had come—as fleet
As Lucifer's when he was driven
By flaming sword away from heaven—
But now the Furies seem aflame
As he bethinks him of his shame:
His brain's on fire, his senses reel
As ocean tides around him steal.

The tides now close around his feet
Like licking tongues, that long to meet
Around the writhing victim's stake
And lap his blood their thirst to slake:
—" The end's the same: by fire or water
Death ends the pangs of selfish martyr
Or blameless captive, Death ends it all,
There is no hell!"—he madly cried,
" Save hell on earth without my bride!
There is no heaven, save that of power
And rank, and wealth, and beauty's dower.
Aha! no mortal man shall gloat
With victor's pride and rival's hate,
Over the fallen chieftain's fate:
Whose fame's as wide as is the sea
Which offers sepulture to me!
Life hath no longer charms, when I,

Who cannot rule, and scorn to fly,
Am witness to *his* victory !
'Tis but a leap, one plunge—no more,
And all thy troubles, life, are o'er !
I'll die as Adelantado !"
And then he turned to curse his foe ;
Nor cloud e'er shrouded sky with gloom
Portending wilder, louder blast
Of thunder, crossing heaven fast,
Nor vivid lightning write the doom
Of vessels bending 'neath the gale,—
Than did the frowns that lowered now
Upon his swarthy face turned pale.
Turned pale? for what? he lists: the sea
Sounds to him like a lullaby.

*   *   *   *   *   *

He saw it gliding fast from view
And tenantless ! his bride's canoe—
—"Sweet Thronatiska, my own ! my own !
Too true ! too true, alas ! my own !"
Then fiercely grew Coacoochee's wrath
As he resumed his lonely path.

Fast strode the chief to the Wild-cat's lair *

* Coacoochee in the Seminole tongue, signifies " Wild-cat."

And warriors crowd around him there—-
A hundred braves—whose savage glare
From angry eyes and painted faces
Grows fiercer as his ire increases—
Nor faggots heaped on forest fire
Burn fiercer than did savage ire,
When Coacoochee, their young chief,
With blazing eyes told of his grief
Which made the Indian women wail,—
Nor did he cease when ceased this tale,
But quick appealed, with hatred's art,
Lover's passion, and chieftain's heart,
That they should do the Indian's part,
And rid the earth of all the men
Who had so many Indians slain!

The amber light rests on the hills
As twilight shadows fill the vales,
While dusky forms glide forward slow,
As Catholics to chapel go.
The *Miserere* has been sung,
The fragrant censer upward swung;
The *"Aves"* are said—and the Priest
Honors our Savior's sacred feast.
Magnolia flowers, white as snow,
Sway over those who come and go;
And, bearding trees, the hanging moss

Waves to the comers weird salute,
As those who go make sign of cross
On breast or forehead.   The whip-poor-will
Sounds warning note from yonder hill:
And echoes now the vesper-bell
From mission church.   Close by, a rill
Winds gently through the forest deep ˙
Where violets and daisies sleep.
Again, they hear the whip-poor-will,
While every other bird is still,
And scarce is heard the ocean's sound.

The vesper bird flies near the ground,
Spreading its wings with mournful cries,
As if to warn of sorrow's birth,
Then, lights, and flutters near the earth:
But, startled, soon it wings its way
To owlet haunts behind the day.

Mysterious bird, hast lost thy nest?
What hidden grief disturbs thy breast?
Hast lost thy mate?   Do angels weep
When loved ones here disturb their sleep
By grievous sins?   Ominous bird
Bird of the eve, what hast thou heard?

Now all are gone; with reverent care
The priest opens the holy book
And kneels alone in fervent prayer—
Nor sounds the swift stiletto-stroke,
When women fall, for not a shriek
Tells how the savage Indians wreak
Their fatal vengeance!

A hundred forms around him go
With threat'ning looks—nor trace of woe
Saddens the face upturned in prayer,
Nor do they see a trace of fear.
He turned, arose,—saw eyes of hate,
Crossed arms on breast, and faced his fate;
His features changed—'twas but with grief—
Then Father Corpa blessed their chief:
From group to group he turned his eyes,
Saw not a friend, but heard their cries.

Again he looked—then prayed to heaven,
Prayed that their sin might be forgiven—
Then gently raised his pious head
And pointing upward calmly said:
—"The Great Spirit, whose eyes descry
Our ev'ry thought, dwells in the sky;
To ev'ry soul a star is given!
To light the glowing path of heaven;—

A star like that of Bethlehem!"
He paused—resumed—and glanced at them:
—"No rootlet bursts its bonds in Spring,
No plant, nor flower, nor living thing:
No rivulet, nor cloud, nor light,
That is not known to Him to-night.

He scarce had ceased when hatchet fell
And, crashing through the good Priest's skull
Left him a corpse—then all was still:
A hundred forms, like phantoms, stand,
Until a whoop calls forth the band
To strew with human wrecks the path
Which vengeance blazes with its wrath!

*   *   *   *   *   *

Not as a Nun was she arrayed,
Though white the veil which Léonore
Upon that sweet occasion wore;
Nor were the nuptials long delayed,
The convent bells announced the hour
When convent lost its sweetest flower:
For Count Ribault looked now with pride
Upon his fair and lovely bride.
The mellow light of evening sun

Illumed the Western horizon,
As Léonore, in bridal dress,
Seemed blessed at last with happiness.

With stooping form and long white hair,
And broken accents, Laudonnière
With trembling gesture blessed the pair;
While soldiers knelt on ev'ry side
As knelt Count Ribault and his bride,
—"God bless ye, my children! may more
Than bliss be yours forevermore!"

A silence deep ensued again
And stoic Indians viewed the scene
With looks impassive: one—the chief—
With accents eloquent but brief,
Thus spake when the old vet'ran ceased;
—"'Twas my hand, chieftain, that released
Thy bended form from dungeon rack—
I owed the debt—I've paid it back,
This is not why Coacoochee speaks,
Nor is it treasure that he seeks;
Nor would he mar this happy scene
If Death would let him speak again."

The young chief paused as if to rest:
Bright ornaments were on his breast,

And heron plumes adorned his crest;
Like Nemesis with vengeant mood,
But waning strength, Coacoochee stood,—
They saw a scalp-lock in his belt,
And scalping-knife, blood-red to hilt!

Glancing around the hall, he said:
—"Coacoochee has avenged the dead!
I saw the Spanish soldiers arm
And heard them plotting deeds of harm;
I heard Menendez tell them where
The "Wild-cat's" trail led to his lair
Beneath the lowest cells; 'twas there
The Spaniards chained Laudonnière!

"I saw Menendez by thee disarmed,
I saw him pass forth free, unharmed—
I heard him give his word to thee
To cross with all his men the sea:
And when I heard him bid his men
To fire this castle and fight again,
I thought again of Indian slaves
And Indian sufferings and graves;
And then of all the countless woes
Heaped on my race by cruel foes!
Enough—we sought them—found them—and
Menendez fell beneath my hand!"

The young chief reeled, sank on his side
And like a Gladiator died.

The Indians entered by the stair
Just when the kneeling bridal pair
Were blessed, and stood in silence near,
While he thus spoke to Laudonnière.

Thus did their trials end; and they
Lived long upon the tropic shore
Where sweet geraniums in full bloom
Grew in profusion near their home:
The fig, the grape, and pomegranate—
With luscious fruit, red-ripe and sweet,—
And trailing, rosy eglantine
Greeted the fragrant wild woodbine;
And fruit, in clusters fair to see,
Swayed over them from orange tree.

Before them lay the ocean beach
Where great white billows leap and reach
And sport like children, while the sea
Uplifts its arms to greet the day;
Behind, the town of Augustine—
As quaint a town as e'er was seen—
And, far as eye could see, the blue
Of mighty ocean charmed the view.

'Tis there one sees how balmy eve
Doth make the sun its traces leave
In golden trails athwart the skies,
Till orange into amber dies;
And then the heavens wide assume
The loveliest cerulean bloom,
Which down the twilight vales of night
Smiles on the earth with mellow light.

'Tis there the moon, like lamp of gold
High-hung amid the massive fold
Of night-clouds in the azure sky,
Keeps sentry watch. 'Twas there her smile
So radiant, so free from guile,—
And naïve as an infant's smile,—
Greeted his own, which looked with pride
Upon his lovely Southern bride.
And angels seemed to hover o'er
The happy home of Léonore.

*   *   *   *   *   *

Home of the exile! hail to thee,
Thou fairest land of liberty!
One century hath passed alone,
Yet it has welded into one

Thy varied peoples; and each race
And sect, and faith, finds welcome place.
Each one for all, all for each one,
Each citizen his country's son,
Each man a citizen and free :
The eyes of all humanity
Are turned, America, to thee!
Beacon of liberty! thy form
Far lights the waters 'mid the storm ;
Goddess of Freedom, lift thy hand
And summon exiles to this land ;
For wars may come, and wars may go,
And human currents ebb and flow
But, Rock of Ages, like to thee
Is this bright sun-land of the free!

THE END.

www.ingramcontent.com/pod-product-compliance
Lightning Source LLC
Chambersburg PA
CBHW020803020726
47495CB00008B/2564